HEREAFTER

AADITYA NANDAN

PROLOGUE

Nathaniel, a 16-year-old, tragically died in a car accident. When his spirit awakened, he found himself lying lifeless on his deathbed, watching his family cry as the doctor broke the heartbreaking news.

Amidst this scene, Nathaniel noticed his childhood friend James, who often appeared in his dreams, standing by a glowing portal. James extended his hand, and Nick felt compelled to follow him into the mysterious gateway. On the other side, he discovered Aquamortis, James's home, now under the tyrannical rule of the evil King Methamis. James revealed that Nathaniel was the only one who could save Aquamortis from Methamis' dark grip.

ABOUT THE AUTHOR

Greetings! I am Aaditya Nandan, and I'm from Prayagraj, Uttar Pradesh. I'm a 14-year-old 9th grader from India. Other than writing stories, I like music very much. Actually, an album that I listened to heavily inspired the concept of this book. Besides music, I enjoy photography, playing the guitar, and basketball, writing poems and songs, polaroids, and collecting keychains. I'd like to thank my parents

and my sister for
encouraging me to write
and finally publish my
very first book. I look
forward to
writing more and more.

ACKNOWLEDGEMENT

I am deeply grateful to everyone who supported me throughout the creation of this book, especially my parents and my sister who deeply encouraged me to write this book throughout the journey.

HEREAFTER

AADITYA NANDAN

HEREAFTER

CHAPTER 1: *HOSPITAL BED*

When Nathaniel awoke, he found himself in a hospital bed, surrounded by an ethereal lightness that seemed to separate him from his physical form. The lightness enveloped him, creating a surreal atmosphere that made everything appear dreamlike and

otherworldly. Looking
down, he saw his own body
lying still on the bed, a
sight that left him
bewildered yet fully
conscious. The stillness
of his body contrasted
sharply with the
vividness of his
awareness, adding to his
confusion. As he ventured
out of the hospital room,
he overheard the
devastating news being
conveyed to his family,
witnessing his father's
heart-wrenching reaction.
The sight of his father's
grief struck him deeply,
making the situation feel
even more surreal.

Struggling to comprehend
his surreal state, he
attempted to dismiss it
as a mere nightmare, only
to confront the
undeniable truth as he
observed his lifeless
body on the monitor. The
monitor displayed the
flat line, confirming the
reality of his passing.
Embracing the reality of
his passing, he was
suddenly confronted by
the appearance of a door,
revealing a familiar
silhouette - James, an
angel from his childhood
dreams. The door seemed
to materialize out of
nowhere, and the sight of

James brought a sense of familiarity and comfort. With reassuring words, James extended his hand to Nathaniel, offering a passage to a destination beyond, assuring him that this was not the end. James' presence and words provided a sense of peace and acceptance. Without hesitation, Nathaniel accepted the offer, taking James' hand as they ventured through the portal together. The portal shimmered with light, and as they stepped through, Nathaniel felt a sense of

calm and anticipation for
what lay ahead.

CHAPTER 2: *THE PORTAL*

As Nathaniel stepped through the mystical portal, he found himself abruptly immersed in a vast ocean. The water enveloped him, it's cool embrace was both soothing and disorienting. Looking up, he saw a dark storm, clouds swirling overhead, unleashing torrents of rain that seemed to have no end. The tempestuous atmosphere mirrored the tumultuous journey that lay ahead. Surprisingly, Nathaniel discovered that he could breathe underwater, a realization that made sense as he realized he was no longer alive. In the depths, a glimmer of light caught his attention, leading him to a tunnel that seemed to stretch into a dark heaven.

Within this ethereal world, Nathaniel encountered James, who warmly greeted him as he explained that they were in Aquamortis, a place where souls resided after completing their earthly lives. James proceeded to recount the unfortunate takeover of Aquamortis by Methamis, the prince of Crimsonia, who had used unfair means to seize power. Methamis had even slain the queen, resulting in the loss of magical abilities for all inhabitants. As James shared these crucial details, he noticed a bright spark in Nathaniel's dark green eyes, leaving him momentarily stunned.

Taking Nathaniel to the main courtroom, James introduced him to Andrew

Raithen Ford, the closest noble to the late queen. They considered Andrew as the potential next king, but he declined the offer, expressing his desire to preserve the queen's power unless a worthy successor with the blessing of another God emerged.

James then revealed the significance of the spark in Nathaniel's eyes, prompting a change in Andrew's reaction. Without hesitation, Andrew rushed out of the courtroom and mounted a horse, heading towards

the Fort of Vision.
James, too, procured a
horse and urged Nathaniel
to join him. Without a
second thought, Nathaniel
accepted the invitation,
and together they
followed Andrew's lead.

CHAPTER 3: *FORT OF VISION*

Upon reaching the fort of vision, Andrew swiftly dismounted his horse and dashed towards the gate. Nathaniel observed that the gate lacked any locks or handles. Suddenly, Andrew began muttering loudly, causing the rain to intensify. A bolt of lightning struck an angel statue atop the fort, its light reflecting through the amethyst walls and creating an intricate pattern. To their astonishment, this pattern summoned a massive book on a grand lectern. The scene appeared surreal, almost otherworldly.

As the gates of the fort swung open, James and Andrew entered first, beckoning Nathaniel to follow. Stepping inside, Nathaniel found the entire place adorned with mirrors, giving the illusion of an expansive space. However, the only object within was a solitary lectern upon which an ancient book rested.

Eagerly, Andrew hurried towards the book, scanning its pages with haste. His excitement was palpable as he exclaimed, "There must be something here, I just know it. The queen said this would happen. I'm certain we can find something to prove it!" Nathaniel, bewildered by the unfolding events, turned to James for guidance.

After a moment of anticipation, Andrew's search yielded results.

He found what he had been
seeking and turned to
Nathaniel, his excitement
causing him to shake with
fervor. Nathaniel, now
even more perplexed,
displayed his confusion
through his expression,
seeking clarification
from James; who
immediately sensed that
Nathaniel, was finding it
difficult, to comprehend
the happenings, James
took Nathaniel, to the
past, historical events,
to clear his confusion.

CHAPTER 4: *HISTORY*

Andrew proceeded to recount the tale of Queen Ruby, a revered and courageous ruler of Aquamortis. She was known for her humility, fierce dedication to her kingdom, and the profound respect she commanded from her subjects. The people of Aquamortis held her in such high regard and they were willing to make great sacrifices to ensure her safety and happiness.

Aquamortis thrived under Queen Ruby's reign until the fateful day when Methamis, the prince of Crimsonia, sent a message in a bottle. In his message, Methamis expressed a desire to end the rivalry between the two kingdoms and apologized for the actions of his ancestors. Queen Ruby, always seeking peace, extended an invitation to Methamis and the royal family of Crimsonia for a dinner, hoping to mend the strained relations between their realms.

The dinner began
harmoniously, with both
kingdoms engaging in
amicable conversation.
However, tragedy struck
when Queen Ruby consumed
a glass of champagne
offered by Methamis as a
gesture of friendship.
She immediately felt a
peculiar sensation in her
throat, witnessing white
foam emerge from her
mouth. At that moment,
she caught sight of
Methamis laughing
maliciously before
collapsing. Unbeknownst
to Queen Ruby, Methamis
had worn a magical ring
passed down through his

lineage. The ring contained a hidden compartment that held a potent poison, capable of inducing a deep, eternal slumber in the immortal queen. Only the death of the ring's opener could awaken her.

As Queen Ruby collapsed, her guards rushed to her side, suspecting Methamis and his family's involvement. However, before they could retaliate, Methamis employed his powers to wash away everyone within the castle, including his own family, unleashing

his aqua strength, which
had passed on to him, as
a lineage.

Methamis possessed
extraordinary abilities
derived from the four
elements of life: fire,
water, earth, and wind,
the water element being
his self. He unleashed
his powers to eliminate
any opposition, driven by
his jealousy and
resentment towards his
sister, Margaret, who had
been appointed the queen
of Crimsonia instead of
him. His parents
recognized her worthiness
due to her fierce nature,

while Methamis merely
boasted of his pride.

Methamis knew he could
not kill Queen Ruby, so
devised a plan to cast
her into an eternal
slumber. By doing so, he
aimed to strip her of her
rightful throne, allowing
him to rule over
Aquamortis. This desire
stemmed from his longing
to rule his
kingdom, Crimsonia.

CHAPTER 5: *CHAMBER OF POWER*

After expelling everyone, he swiftly constructed a chamber by drawing in all the tears shed in that kingdom with his winding powers. This action even revived and drew out the tears of their ancestors from the ground. He then uttered a spell, "I DECLARE MYSELF AS THE NEW KING OF AQUAMORTIS, AND NOW I ORDER THE POWER OF EVERY ANGEL, NYMPH, SIRENS, FAERIE, AND EVERY

OTHER CREATURE TO BE
STORED IN THE CHAMBER OF
POWERS. As he raised his
wand in the sky, all the
powers were drawn out of
every creature, and
within seconds, the power
was in his hands. He
stored it in the chamber
of powers and closed it.
He then took control of
the workers of the
castles to work for him
and destroyed the castle
to bits. Since then, he
has been ruling the
kingdom, however, James,
Andrew, and a few others
managed to avoid coming
in contact with the beam
of possessions and

thankfully didn't become contortionists for Methamis. They watched their castle crumbling down in front of their eyes. The very same castle that they built together with the Queen, with the sacrifice of their blood, sweat, and tears.

After narrating all this, Andrew told Nathaniel that James saw a bright light in his eyes, which was unusual as all the powers of Aquamortis were in the chamber of powers. But the shine in Nathaniel's eyes revealed that there was still a spark of magic left in Aquamortis, and that spark was in Nathaniel. Usually, when a dead being is brought to Aquamortis, most of them are not able to pass in the ocean and have to return to the mortal world and thus remain trapped in the cycle of death, and the person is reborn. But something was special about Nathaniel, which made him survive the ocean. Then Andrew told Nathaniel that he was the only being who could save the kingdom of Aquamortis and such was

the prophecy of their
Queen.

Nathaniel was astonished
after hearing about the
spark. After reading and
keeping the book, they
rode off to the main
courtroom, where Andrew
told Nathaniel that to
save Aquamortis, he
needed to get the
remaining fossils left.
Then he asked Augusta, a
siren angel, to take him
to the ambassador of the
siren kingdom for further
information.

CHAPTER 6: *SIRENS*

To begin their journey, Augusta took Nathaniel in the water oasis shower. Together with a group of other sirens, Augusta carefully cleansed Nathaniel, removing all the muck from the earth and the sea. The sirens then proceeded to impart their knowledge of the mystical and magical aquatic life to Nathaniel, teaching him the intricacies and specialties of their underwater realm.

Augusta took the lead, guiding Nathaniel through the enchanting nymph lagoon. The lagoon was a breathtaking sight, filled with a diverse array of nature. Each pond was shrouded in a delicate mist that, when touched, felt like the softest gold. The air was filled with the gentle fluttering of cold wings, and every flower exuded a captivating scent reminiscent of pomegranate. The water in the ponds possessed an unusual density, yet the sirens moved through it effortlessly, seemingly unaffected. Nathaniel couldn't help but feel a mix of awe, beauty, and strangeness as he took in the surreal surroundings. After their exploration, Augusta led Nathaniel to meet the ambassador of the Siren kingdom.

Nathaniel was coldly greeted by Agatha, the head siren. With an intriguing undertone in her voice, she uttered, "The melody of a siren is not a cry for the crown, but the euphoria of extreme felicity." Nathaniel was puzzled by her cryptic statement, and it showed on his face. Sensing his confusion, Agatha beckoned him to step into the light. Augusta then proceeded to explain everything that had transpired to the ambassador. Agatha, in turn, revealed to Nathaniel that her powers no longer resided within her, but there was a prophecy that a soul would find her, who would restore her powers, along with other residents of Aquamortis and now they know that it's him, who would restore their magical powers.

To achieve this, he would
need to vanquish the
cruel Methamis and embark
on a journey through a
mysterious cave, where
the third fossil awaited.
This fossil held the key
to saving the kingdom
from Methamis' clutches.
With that, Agatha
concluded that they had
shared all the necessary
information.

Nathaniel's confusion
deepened upon hearing
about a fossil, and it
was evident on his face.
Queen Agatha noticed his
perplexity and proceeded

to explain that, to save
the kingdom of
Aquamortis, they required
a total of four fossils.
These fossils,
representing the elements
of water, soil, fire, and
wind, hold the power
necessary to unlock the
chamber of power and
restore balance to the
kingdom. She further
revealed that two knights
had already embarked on
the quest for the first
two fossils, successfully
obtaining them, but they
had not returned. It was
now Nathaniel's
responsibility to
retrieve the third

fossil, and the fourth
and final one would be
obtained once Methamis
was defeated.

Curious about his role
and what set him apart
from the previous
knights, Nathaniel
questioned Agatha's
confidence in his ability
to find the third fossil
and bring it, along with
the other two knights,
safely to the ruins of
the main courtroom.
Agatha admitted that she
couldn't be certain of
his success, but she
expressed hope, as
magical powers resided

within Nathaniel, unlike most creatures of Aquamortis. This opportunity couldn't be overlooked.

Understanding the weight of the task before him, Nathaniel wholeheartedly accepted the challenge, expressing his unwavering commitment to saving the Kingdom of Aquamortis. Agatha then proceeded to enlighten him about the magical cave, where his journey
would truly begin.

CHAPTER 7: *RELICS*

Queen Agatha, with a sense of trepidation, confided in Nathaniel about her limited understanding of the enigmatic and mystical cave that lay ahead of him. Delving into the annals of history, she recounted the ancient prophecies of Lady Heather Woke, a revered priestess, who had foreseen the difficult fate of Aquamortis at the hands of a malevolent entity. The prophecies detailed the intricate stages associated with the magical crystal fossils, alluding to the presence of illusions, souls, and evil eyes that turned into deformed figures if disturbed within the cave, indicating that Nathaniel would not be venturing into its depths alone.

Expanding on the daunting nature of the cave, Queen Agatha expounded on the myriad obstacles and bewitched levels that lay in wait, ultimately leading to a staircase that would guide Nathaniel to the coveted fossil. However, she cautioned that the path to the fossil would be fraught with further challenges. Upon ascending the staircase, Nathaniel would be confronted by a mysterious lake, the means of traversing that lake remained shrouded in uncertainty. Despite this, Queen Agatha expressed unwavering confidence that he would be fine because of this one blue aquamarine liquid which he will be provided later, and that liquid will protect him and help him reach the fossil, with its mystical powers.

Upon finally reaching the fossil, Nathaniel would be granted a fleeting 13 seconds to deploy the protective blue aquamarine liquid around himself and the fossil, shielding them from the disconcerting gazes of the souls embedded within the walls encircling the lake. Within this brief window, Nathaniel would need to secure the fossil and discern vital clues to find his escape. The chances of failing to find a way out within the allotted time remained a disquieting enigma, instilling a sense of apprehension in Nathaniel because if he didn't get the crystal and leave in time, he would be trapped inside the void forever without any way of escaping. Nevertheless, resolute in his determination, he remained steadfast in his commitment to the salvation of Aquamortis.

CHAPTER 8: *GLOBED*

After recounting everything to Nathaniel, Queen Agatha descended from her throne and walked towards the eastern part of the ruined castle room, where a large red and tattered curtain concealed something. It almost appeared to be a miniature throne beneath it. However, as Queen Agatha removed the curtain, the object's shape seemed to transform, resembling a snow globe. This transformation didn't surprise Nathaniel, considering the series of astonishments he had experienced in the past hours. Lost in his thoughts, he suddenly snapped back to reality and realized that he was inside the snow globe. This revelation startled him, evident from his frightened eyes, which Queen Agatha noticed.

"Don't worry, you will be fine," she reassured him. Curious, Nathaniel asked why he was chosen to undergo this process. Queen Agatha reminded him that he and a select few beings of Methamis possessed unique powers within them, making them capable of shape-shifting and mystical qualities that no longer remained within the inhabitants of Aquamortis since the rule of Methamis

As soon as she finished speaking, everything around Nathaniel went blank. A light from the top of the globe descended and struck him directly on the head, causing intense pain. Though he refrained from exclaiming, a groan

escaped him. Just when he thought it was over and wouldn't happen again, four more lights struck him. The pain became unbearable, but then eight more lights struck his chest. He screamed, although no one could hear him. After enduring all of this, he suddenly felt lifted
from the surface.

He was still in great pain and agony when he was struck with a barrage of armor pieces: first, a chest plate, then tasses, followed by a helmet, a knee piece, a shoulder piece, chainmail gloves, and a pair of sabatons. The final item was an opal-shaped locket containing an aquamarine-colored glowing liquid. Nathaniel surmised that this was the liquid Queen Agatha had previously mentioned, though she offered no further explanation about it. After this ordeal, he was unceremoniously dropped to the surface of the globe once more. Nathaniel struggled to his feet, bracing himself for another wave of pain, but to his surprise, it was gone. He barely had

time to process this
before he was struck
again by a beam of light.
This time, however, it
didn't hurt. Instead, as
soon as the light touched
him, his armor lit up
with a vibrant red glow.
As he inspected his newly
illuminated armor, he
realized he was no longer
inside the globe. He was
standing before Queen
Agatha. "There you go,"
she said, a satisfied
smile on her face. "I'm
so happy this was
successful. Nathaniel
felt a surge of happiness
as well, not only because
he had proven useful to

them, but also because
his determination to save
this dimension had grown
even stronger. He stood
taller, the red glow of
his armor reflecting his
renewed resolve, ready to
face whatever
challenges lay ahead.

CHAPTER 9: *THE ABYSS OF TRACE*

After Nathaniel armed himself, Queen Agatha instructed Augusta to take him to a well-known Well of Vision. Nathaniel was about to inquire about the well, but Queen Agatha interrupted him and wished him the best for what was to come, assuring him of her prayers for him.

Augusta took Nathaniel's hand and guided him

directly to the well. Along the way, Nathaniel asked the questions he couldn't ask Queen Agatha and learned that the well served as the entrance to the cave. However, before entering the cave, he would face some potentially harmful shots, so he needed to be prepared.

As they conversed, they arrived at a beautifully ruined Roman-style architecture that captivated their attention. They entered the center of the ruin, where Augusta informed

Nathaniel, "Perfect! Only thirteen minutes until the well opens."

"Opens? What does that mean?" Nathaniel inquired.

"Oh, I thought you were informed about this at the Fort of Vision. Anyway, the well appears every day when the moonlight hits the diamond carved on the floor, passing through the opening of the ruin at the top," Augusta explained.

"I see. How much time is left for the light to strike the diamond?" Nathaniel asked.

"Just a few minutes, as I mentioned. We are just in time," Augusta replied. She then looked at the moon and exclaimed, "Oh look, it's happening already!" She pointed Nathaniel's attention to the top of the ruin, where they witnessed the light gradually reaching the diamond. As soon as it did, a strange gloom enveloped the light, taking the shape of a well. Augusta touched it, and it solidified. She then gestured for Nathaniel to jump in. Nathaniel glanced at Augusta once and dived headfirst into the well.

After descending into the well, he was momentarily blinded by a sudden flash of bright green light. When his vision returned, he found himself surrounded by numerous moths. As he fell to the ground, he realized he was lying on a grassy path and promptly blacked out.

Distant and distorted screams woke him up, emanating from a massive rock. Nathaniel approached the rock, gently touching it. The rock slid to the west, revealing a hallway. The hallway seemed endless, but Nathaniel decided to proceed. After walking about fifty steps, he contemplated turning back to find another way to reach the fossil. However, as soon as this thought crossed his mind, he felt himself sinking into the ground, being pulled by quicksand. Nathaniel struggled to escape, but just as his face was about to touch the sand, he closed his eyes. A few seconds later, he found himself falling and soon landed on another grassy path. "How many times do I have to fall like this to reach that fossil?" Nathaniel wondered. Nevertheless, he was pleased to discover that he had come closer to the fossil, as the aquamarine liquid in his locket glowed even brighter.

Brushing off some sand and getting back on his feet, Nathaniel looked up

to behold a mesmerizing
and mystical lush cave.
It was filled with
various forms of nature,
including bioluminescent
plants, waterfalls, and
even lava. Glowing
insects fluttered around,
captivating his
attention. The grassy
path he stood on began to
move forward, allowing
Nathaniel to observe the
enchanting surroundings
in greater detail.

As the grassy path
advanced, Nathaniel
marveled at the diverse
nature surrounding him.
However, he soon noticed

the glowing plants losing
their light, the flying
insects falling to the
ground and burning to
death, the water ceasing
to flow, and the grass
losing its vibrant green
color. The once
mesmerizing view
transformed into a
nightmarish scene.

The grassy path halted as
it reached the other side
of the cave. Nathaniel
stepped off the path and
looked back, witnessing
the cave engulfed in a
brutal and horrific
blaze. He turned away and
resumed walking forward.

Eventually, he spotted a small opening in the wall and entered. At this point, the liquid in his locket glowed so brightly that the locket itself appeared as a ball of light on his chest.

Surprisingly, after walking for approximately seven minutes, he encountered a staircase leading down to a rocky ground. Just before him lay a small body of water with stones, leading to the sacred fossil. Descending the stairs, he saw the fossil right in front of him.

As Nathaniel approached, his locket glowed even brighter. Suddenly, a red light illuminated a curved path, resembling an invisible string. Nathaniel assumed he had to pass through the watery path without touching the red string. To confirm his assumption, he removed the locket from its soft string and threw it at one of the red lines. Nothing happened when the locket string touched the red string, but a few seconds later, it started burning red, summoning at

least seventy pairs of
eyes that stared at
Nathaniel. He recalled
these eyes as the evil
eyes Queen Agatha had
warned him about.

Now came the crucial part
of Nathaniel's journey to
obtain the fossil. He had
to act swiftly, crossing
the water while spilling
the liquid before the
eyes reached him. Wiping
the sweat from his
forehead, he took a deep
breath and ran for it.
Stepping on the first
rock, he heard the
distorted screams, but
they seemed more distant.

Dodging the first red string, he glanced back at his left hand, only to see it detach and tear from his body. Terrified, he continued running. Passing several more rocks, he felt his right hand fall off, but he didn't look back, knowing what had happened. He kept running and evading the red strings, moving from step to step until he reached the fifteenth rock. As he placed his foot on it, the rock trembled, causing Nathaniel to fall just centimeters away from a red string that blazed

away a strand of his
hair. The upper surface
of the cave began to
collapse.

Still lying down,
exhausted, Nathaniel's
thoughts turned to his
locket, which was in his
right hand. Panic struck
him as he realized that
his right hand had fallen
off while running. He
hastily examined his
hands and was surprised
to find them intact, with
the locket resting in the
palm of his right hand.
It was truly astonishing,
as he had witnessed both
of his hands falling off

with his own eyes. He
then realized that it was
one of the illusions
Queen Agatha had warned
him about.

Relieved, Nathaniel let
out a sigh of relief.
Looking up, he understood
that he needed to spill
the aquamarine liquid.
Just as this thought
crossed his mind, he
noticed the deformed
figures glaring at him
with deep frowns on their
faces. He swiftly got to
his feet, and at that
moment, the distorted
figures' eyes turned a
dark burgundy color and

began advancing toward Nathaniel. However, he managed to spill the liquid in the nick of time as instructed by Queen Agatha.

The liquid illuminated the ground, glowing brightly. Within seconds, a transparent aquamarine curved wall materialized in front of Nathaniel, covering him and the fossil. He attempted to grab the fossil, but it remained stuck to the table on which it was placed. As the thirteen seconds elapsed, the ground beneath him vanished, leaving only the table suspended in the black void. Clinging to the fossil, Nathaniel and the fossil fell into the void.

He believed that his journey to save Aquamortis had come to an end and that he had failed. The impact of the fall shook Nathaniel to his core, causing him genuine pain, unlike the previous falls he had experienced. Everything turned pitch black until a blinding white light engulfed him. When his vision returned, he first

looked at the fossil,
which remained in perfect
condition. Then, he
noticed a spotlight
shining on him, the sole
source of light
in the dark void.

CHAPTER 10: *FILM REEL*

"Nathaniel… yes, I know your name… but do you know mine?" echoed a deep voice, reverberating ominously within the cave's dark, damp confines.

"I am Lord Methamis, the sovereign of Aquamortis. But that's not of immediate importance. What matters now is how you managed to penetrate the depths of my mind and enter my memories. You were destined to be lost in the void, never to return. Yet, here you are, and now, I cannot prevent you from witnessing my past. So, take a seat and prepare to experience the torment I have endured."

As Methamis concluded his foreboding statement, water began to rapidly fill the void, rising swiftly and drowning Nathaniel within moments. The force of the water was overwhelming, knocking the precious fossil from Nathaniel's

grasp. A tornado formed
with sudden ferocity, and
Nathaniel found himself
utterly helpless, his
body tossed around
violently. His attempts
to scream were futile in
the deafening maelstrom,
his voice swallowed by
the raging vortex.

Abruptly, Nathaniel was
flung into the eye of the
tornado. There, distorted
and shadowy figures
seized his limbs, holding
him captive. Before him,
a film reel started to
play, illuminating the
darkness with flickering

images of Methamis'
memories.

The first memory unfolded
in a stark hospital
scene. A woman was in the
throes of birthing a
child, her agonized
screams echoing through
the halls. Outside the
delivery room, a child
and a man waited
anxiously. This woman was
Methamis' mother, giving
birth to his younger
sister, Margaret. The
waiting child was young
Methamis, accompanied by
his father. Just moments
after the screaming
ceased, a nurse emerged,

jubilantly announcing,
"It's a girl!" Methamis
and his father erupted in
joy, and nine-year-old
Methamis began to chant,
"I have a younger sister
now!" over and over, his
excitement uncontainable.

After returning home with
the mother and the
newborn, the family
lavished attention and
care on the baby. Despite
his love for his sister,
Methamis often felt
neglected, a shadow in
his own home. This sense
of abandonment festered,
turning his affection
into a secret hatred. In

his loneliness, he frequently retreated to the solace of a library. There, he stumbled upon a book detailing the experiences of death and the afterlife. Fascinated, he delved deeper into the subject, his obsession growing with each book he read. One fateful day, he discovered a story about a God who sacrificed his mother to the devil to gain eternal wealth and charm. This tale captivated Methamis, and he resolved to perform a similar ritual, intending to sacrifice his sister

in exchange for eternal
riches.

For a week, he
painstakingly gathered
the required materials
for the ritual. On a full
red moon night, he
surreptitiously crept to
the attic of Aquamortis'
castle and meticulously
set up the ritual as
described in the book.
Methamis then went to his
parents' room, stealthily
took his sister from her
cradle, and returned to
the attic. He lit exactly
34 candles, arranging
them in a perfect circle
beneath the ritual setup.

He placed his sister in the center of the circle, ensuring the moonlight touched her forehead. He began chanting the incantations to summon the demon.

As he neared the spell's completion, the candle flames blazed bright red, and the moonlight acted like a razor, etching the demon's symbol onto his sister's forehead. Her agonized cries echoed through the castle, awakening their parents. They rushed to the attic, where Methamis' father forcefully pulled him

away, and his mother
hastily grabbed the baby,
wiping the blood from her
forehead. Methamis'
father, enraged, began to
scold and beat him,
demanding to know why he
had attempted such a
horrendous act. When
Methamis explained, his
father's fury
intensified. He ordered
Methamis to his room,
promising severe
consequences.

Methamis fled to his
room, tears streaming
down his face. His sorrow
was unending, he just
could not stop his tears.

He wept until his tears
flooded the room.
Desperate, he swam to the
door, banging on it and
crying out for help.
Nathaniel, witnessing all
this on a screen, was
overwhelmed and began to
feel sorry and cry as
well. Suddenly, the
screen shattered, and the
tears flooded the void,
engulfing Nathaniel
completely.

Nathaniel felt himself
drowning and
simultaneously his lungs
also started burning, as
he struggled to breathe.
He swam frantically, his

screams muted by the water, until he blacked out from sheer exhaustion.

He awoke on parched land, the fossil lying nearby. Rising to his feet, he retrieved the fossil and turned to a horrifying sight: three knights submerged in marble pillars, each holding a fossil. He approached cautiously, carefully prying the fossil from the first knight's grasp, then from the second. As he took the third fossil, the ground trembled violently, and a fierce thunderstorm erupted, quickly forming a tornado.

Nathaniel was sucked into the tornado, but this time he clung to the fossils with all his strength. The struggle to breathe intensified until he blacked out once more.

When he regained consciousness, Augusta was calling his name, shaking him gently. "You're finally awake! And you even got all three fossils, good job!" she exclaimed. Nathaniel looked around, realizing

he was beside the well he
had jumped into earlier.
He woke up feeling
miserable after hearing
what happened with
Methamis but then elated,
he shouted, "I got them!
I was successful!"

"Yes! You made it! I
can't wait to show this
to Queen Agatha," Augusta
replied, her
excitement matching his.

CHAPTER 11: *VENTURE BACK*

Nathaniel and Augusta rose to their feet, embarking on their journey back to the towering ruins of Queen Agatha. As they retraced their steps, they observed the gradual fading of the enchanted forest's magic.

Augusta expressed her concern, noting the diminishing singing of the forest angels and the reduced flight of the

flying insects. The sight
of the grass growing
paler each day visibly
saddened her, all due to
the absence of magic.

They aimed to reach the
ruin before nightfall, as
the evil air of the night
stirred the creatures in
the wild and emancipated
their dangerous behavior.
These creatures were
known for their penchant
for chewing on wings and
thriving on blood.

Upon reaching a lake that
lay in their path to the
towering ruin, they were
alarmed to find the water

had turned into a bright shade of red. Augusta remarked that this was highly unusual, and as they gazed at the reflection of the moon in the river, they noticed it was tinged with red.

"This isn't a good sign," said Augusta, prompting them to hasten over the bridge towards the ruin.

CHAPTER 12: THE BATTLE OF THE CROWN

Queen Agatha's face lit up with a smile as she witnessed Nathaniel and Augusta's arrival.

"Are you both alright? Did you get it?" she inquired eagerly.

"Yup, we did... Nathaniel did while I waited outside," Augusta replied, with a smirk.

Nathaniel then handed over the three fossils. Queen Agatha couldn't believe her eyes. Finally, she possessed all three fossils. The only remaining task was to defeat Methamis. Once defeated, Nathaniel would retrieve the fourth fossil from Methamis' ashes and place all four fossils in front of the chamber where the powers were trapped. This would unleash the powers and once again, goodness would return.

Nathaniel was then sent to take a rest and

prepare for what awaited them—the impending war. After a few hours of rest, they embarked on their venture towards Methamis' castle.

As Nathaniel and Augusta made their way through the enchanted forest surrounding the towering castle, they couldn't help but notice the continuous fading colors of the forest and the visibly miserable creatures in worse conditions. This saddened them again, especially Augusta. Nevertheless, they continued towards

the castle until they
reached its premises.

Their next challenge was
to enter the castle
without alerting the
guards. In the dead of
night, they searched for
a quieter entrance but
found none without
guards. They wondered if
they would be able to
enter without alerting
the guards and how.
Suddenly, Nathaniel
spotted people entering
the palace in carts. He
called Augusta's
attention to it. Augusta
had a brilliant idea—
those people were mailing

fairies delivering
letters to Methamis from
other kingdoms. They
could disguise themselves
as mail fairies. Augusta
used her remaining powers
to change their
appearance into that of
mailmen. They joined the
mail cart, blending in
with the other fairies.

Passing through the
guards, they successfully
entered the palace. They
quickly hid behind a
pillar as the cart
entered the palace
corridors, unnoticed by
the other mailmen.

As they ventured deeper into the palace, they encountered various enchanted obstacles and security measures. With Augusta's brilliance and Nathaniel's bravery, they swiftly overcame each one.

Finally, Nathaniel and Augusta reached the inner sanctum where the chamber containing the powers was located. They saw the lectern where the four stones needed to be placed. However, as Nathaniel approached, Augusta cried out loudly. Nathaniel turned to see

guards restraining
Augusta and Methamis
himself standing
menacingly. Methamis
summoned more guards, and
a fierce battle ensued.
Nathaniel and Augusta
fought valiantly, holding
their ground against
overwhelming odds.

Amid the intense battle,
as the guards closed in
on Nathaniel and Augusta,
Methamis sat on his
throne, laughing
maliciously. Unknowingly,
Nathaniel's glass-green
eyes flashed, causing the
guards around him to be
knocked back as if some

mystical power unleashed from within his soul. This surprised Nathaniel but not Augusta, who smiled as if she had anticipated it. Methamis grew concerned upon witnessing this.

Seizing the opportunity, Augusta called out to Nathaniel and tossed him an enchantment bottle which Queen Agatha gave her without this knowledge getting to Nathaniel. Augusta looked at him and he suddenly knew what to do—he smashed the bottle on the marble floor, freezing

everyone except him and
Augusta. As the liquid
savored the air, things
started changing, and
step by step, body parts
of the guards and
Methamis started getting
frozen, and eventually
with a loud cry as he
froze to death, his
existence
withered away.

As Methamis' body
withered leaving behind
ashes, Nathaniel quickly
ran up to it to dig in
the fourth fossil.

Augusta gave Nathaniel a
knowing look, and they

approached the lectern.
Nathaniel retrieved the
three fossils from his
leather bag pocket and
placed the four of them
in the correct order. As
he did so, strange sounds
emanated from each
fossil; and all of them
lit up, in four different
colours, representing
fire, water, earth, and
air.

Once the fossils settled
in place on the weathered
lectern, the ground
beneath their feet
trembled. Unexpectedly,
instead of opening, the
chamber's entrance began

to crack. Nathaniel and Augusta exchanged horrified glances, wondering if they had done something wrong. Suddenly, a dazzling array of radiant energy burst forth. Within the chamber, the powers of countless beings, long trapped in time, surged out in a magnificent display of light and sound. Nathaniel and Augusta stood there, enthralled by the power cascading around them.

Nathaniel couldn't contain his excitement and exclaimed quietly, then shouted, "We did it!" He began jumping with joy, while Augusta giggled in response.

CHAPTER 13: THE CROWNING

The ray of power then started to project majestically out of Methamis' palace. Nathaniel and Augusta started to follow it and soon realized that the ray was showing the path to the Main Court Room where Andrew and the others awaited Nathaniel.

On their way back, the change in their surroundings was noticeable and they started cheering. The forest was greener than ever, and the forest creatures were filled with life and the buzz of their wings was eternal music to their ears. They soon reached the main court and the ray of power struck a large crystal on the top, distributing itself all over Aquamortis.

In an instance, every creature who had long been bereft of their powers regained their magic.
As the magical energy surged through the air,

it intertwined with the spirits of the magical creatures of Aquamortis.

The sky resonated with the sound of joy and everything felt complete. The magic array striking the gigantic crystal was the most eternally beautiful thing Nathaniel had ever seen.

Nathaniel and Augusta stood in awe, witnessing the mesmerizing sight of the ray striking the crystal. Queen Agatha along with Queen Ruby walked in on the sight smiling. Everyone cheered as loud as they could and Aquamortis lit up like never before!

Then suddenly the sky turned a deep, ominous shade of red, casting a foreboding shadow over the land. A chilling whisper echoed through the air, hinting at a looming threat yet to be unveiled.
Little did they know, this was just the beginning of a new, perilous journey that awaited them.

They all rushed towards a mountain peak to get a clearer view.

The whispers of an ancient prophecy began to circulate among the people, hinting at a forgotten darkness that threatened to engulf their world once again. Queen Ruby, her eyes filled with terror, knew that the time had come to unearth the long-buried secrets of the land.

www.ingramcontent.com/pod-product-compliance
Lightning Source LLC
Chambersburg PA
CBHW031313130726
47988CB00007B/2824